I hope you enjoy this book.
It's been called the most famous
indian story of all time.
I love to read and hope you
do to.   Stve

GREAT ILLUSTRATED CLASSICS

THE LAST OF THE MOHICANS

James Fenimore Cooper

adapted by
Eliza Gatewood Warren

**Illustrations by
Pablo Marcos Studio**

**BARONET
B·O·O·K·S**

BARONET BOOKS, New York, New York

Contents

About the Author

James Fenimore Cooper lived from 1789 to 1851. He is considered the first important American novelist, and his tale, The *Last of the Mohicans,* has been called the most famous Indian story of all time.

Cooper was the inventor of wilderness adventures as well as sea-romance stories. As a boy growing up in Cooperstown, New York— a village his father, a prominent Quaker landowner, founded—he had daily contact with the Indians on the frontier. The background and characters for many of his novels are drawn from these early impressions.

One of eleven children, Cooper entered Yale University at the age of thirteen, but was expelled for a prank. He went to sea for a time as a cabin boy and joined the navy. When he returned, he married and lived in Cooperstown and later, Scarsdale, New York, where his thirty-year writing career began.

Cooper wrote fifty books including thirty-three novels. His five most famous frontier works are *The Deerslayer, The Last of the Mohicans, The Pathfinder, The Pioneers,* and *The Prairie.* The hero of these novels—a woodsman called at different times Natty Bumppo, Hawkeye, or the Deerslayer—shares many exciting adventures with his Indian friend, Chingachgook, a Mohican chief. This series, called The Leather-Stocking Tales, has been called "an American epic of the expanding frontier."

Other favorite Cooper novels young people read to this day are *The Pilot,* his great sea adventure, and *The Spy,* a tale of the turbulent days of the American Revolution.

A War in the New World

CHAPTER 1

The Long Journey Begins

Our story opens on a hot July day in 1757. It was the third year of the French and Indian War—a war England and France waged for the possession of New World. Both countries were destined to lose that territory, known then as the thirteen colonies.

The setting is upper New York State near the head-waters, or source, of the Hudson River and nearby Lake George and Lake Champlain. Here, in these lush green forests, most of the battles were fought.

The hardy colonists and the trained English soldiers had to conquer the wilderness together before they could meet the French and their Indian allies in battle. But in time, every raging river and rugged mountain pass had been conquered by these newcomers.

Both sides erected forts at strategic points along the battle route, and the surrounding woods were alive with men. The sounds of their marching music rang throughout the rocky glens.

The recent losses of Edward Braddock, the British general, had greatly lowered the colonists' and the soldiers' morale. To make matters worse, countless massacres by barbarous Indians were still vivid in the minds of the frightened settlers. Even the bravest of settlers and soldiers began to doubt the outcome of the war they were fighting.

Therefore, when news reached Fort Edward, south of the fighting, that the French General Montcalm had been seen moving down Lake Champlain with a large army, anxiety mounted among the British and

A British Fort Along the Battle Route

Americans.

The news was delivered to General Webb at Fort Edward by an Indian runner who dashed into camp late one afternoon.

"Colonel Munro will never be able to hold Fort William Henry with only a thousand men," the red man told the soldiers at the gate. "He must have reinforcements immediately."

General Webb, in turn, ordered a detachment of 1,500 men to make the fifteen-mile journey between the two forts. "Prepare to march at dawn!" he directed his aides. And hours of hurried arrangements began.

The next morning, the entire camp watched the departure of their comrades. As the notes of their fifes grew fainter in the distance, the forest appeared to swallow up the whole detachment of 1,500 men.

Outside the general's cabin, three horses were being saddled and loaded for a long trip. They whinnied restlessly and stomped their

General Webb Issues Orders.

hoofs impatiently in the dust. They were waiting to carry Cora and Alice Munro from Fort Edward to Fort William Henry, where they would be reunited with their father, Colonel Munro, the commanding officer at the fort. A British major, Duncan Heyward, would accompany the two women.

Two men watched the loading of the horses with great interest. Their appearance set them apart from the rest of the people at the fort. The white man was of particularly awkward build. His head was large and his shoulders narrow. His arms and legs were long and scrawny. He wore a sky-blue coat with a cape and short skirt and a cocked hat like that of a clergyman. This clothing only made his awkwardness more conspicuous.

The second man was the Indian runner who had brought the news to the fort. His brilliant war-paint made his features savage and repulsive.

The white man and the Indian stared

Watching the Loading of the Horses

intently at the departing group. The two beautiful Munro sisters had mounted their horses. The major sprang lightly into his saddle, and the three rode out of camp.

The Indian rushed by the white man and took the lead in the procession. Seeing him, Alice Munro cried out in dismay, "There's something about that Indian that frightens me, Duncan. What makes you trust him?"

"He's a runner for our army," Heyward answered. "And even though your father once had some trouble with him, he has volunteered to guide us to the fort by an Indian path. We will get there a lot sooner than if we followed the detachment of troops. Don't worry, my dear, he is our friend."

"If he was my father's enemy, perhaps there is cause for me to worry," replied the anxious girl.

But ahead of them, the Indian had stopped and was now pointing out a path that led from the road into the thicket.

The Indian Rushes By.

"This is the way, Alice," said Heyward. "Let us move along without showing any distrust."

"Cora, what do you think?" Alice Munroe asked her sister. "Wouldn't you feel safer traveling with the troops?"

Cora sat frozen in her saddle. "Should we distrust our guide simply because he is a different race?" she said coldly.

Alice didn't hesitate another minute. She gave her horse a small cut of the whip and followed the runner along the dark, tangled path into the woods. The others fell in behind her.

They had ridden only a short distance when a colt, gliding like a deer through the pines, came into view. His rider was none other than the comical man in the sky-blue coat from the fort.

Major Heyward had to suppress a smile at the sight of this ridiculous-looking man. "What can I do for you, my good man?" asked

Following the Runner into the Woods

the major.

Fanning his face with his cocked hat, the stranger replied, "I would like to ride in your pleasant company to Fort William Henry."

"I think you have mistaken your route," the major answered haughtily. "The highway to Lake George is a half-mile behind you."

But their uninvited guest was not put off by the cold reception. "I've been at Fort Edward a week," he replied, "and it's time for a man of my profession to move on."

"Tell me, sir, what is your profession?" asked Heyward.

"I teach music. My specialty is the beautiful psalms of the Bible."

"A singing master!" cried Alice. "Duncan, let this fascinating man join our party." Then, in a whisper, she added, "He would be a friend if we run into trouble."

Heyward nodded in agreement.

The stranger gratefully fell in line with Alice and, as they rode, the two began to sing

The Singing Master Wants To Join the Party.

a psalm in full, sweet melodious tones.

The Indian, who was a short distance ahead of the group, turned and muttered a few words in broken English to Heyward.

The major called over his shoulder, "We must be as quiet as possible on this trip. So you will have to postpone your singing until we are in a safer place."

As he spoke, he peered into the nearby thicket. For just a moment he imagined that some shiny berries were the glistening eye-balls of a prowling savage. But he shrugged it off and rode on steadily behind the Indian guide into the woods.

After the procession had passed, the branches of the thicket parted cautiously. Out from their depths crept an Indian as wild-looking as savage war-paint could make him. There was no mistaking the murderous determination on his darkly painted face as he watched his intended victims disappear into the trees!

A Wild-Looking, Prowling Savage!

Two Friends Talk of Their History.

CHAPTER 2

Lost in the Forest

A few miles away in the same silent forest, on that same July day, an Indian and a white man—a colonial scout—sat talking on the bank of the mighty Hudson River.

Their voices rose and fell as the two friends discussed the history of both their races in the New World and the problems that existed between them. The only other sounds to be heard were the occasional lazy tap of a woodpecker or the dull roar of a distant waterfall.

The Indian was Chingachgook, a chief of the Mohicans, and Hawkeye was the name the Indians had given to the scout whose

23

Christian name was really Natty Bumppo.

"I admit I don't approve of all the things my people have done," said Hawkeye. "But tell me, Chingachgook, according to the red men, what happened when our forefathers first met?"

For a moment Chingachgook remained silent. Then he leaned forward from his seat on the end of a mossy log and spoke with great dignity. "My tribe, the Mohicans, is the grandfather of all Indian nations, and the blood of chiefs runs through my veins. But when the Dutch came and settled New York, they gave my people fire-water. They drank until heaven and earth seemed to meet, and they foolishly thought they had found the Great Spirit. Then they parted with their land. Foot by foot they were driven back from the shore so far into the forest that they began living with the Delaware tribes. And I, a chief, have never seen the Mohican land by the sea or the graves of my forefathers."

Chingachgook Tells of the Mohican Tribe.

Hawkeye was deeply touched at the suffering of his companion. "Where are the Mohicans now?" he asked.

"All my family have departed to the land of the spirits," the Indian went on, "and when I die, my son Uncas will become chief, for he is the last of the Mohicans."

"Uncas is here," said a soft voice. The young warrior walked past them and sat down on the river bank.

"Have you found prints of Iroquois moccasins in these woods?" his father asked him. "Have they dared. . . ?"

"Yes, I have been following their trail," replied the young Indian. "There are about ten of them, hidden like cowards in the bushes."

"That bushy Frenchman, General Montcalm, has sent them down from Canada to spy and murder and steal," said Hawkeye.

Glancing toward the setting sun, Chingachgook replied, "The Iroquois shall be driven like deer from their bushes. Hawkeye,

Uncas, the Last of the Mohicans

let us eat tonight and show them that we are men tomorrow."

"To eat, we must find game," answered Hawkeye. "And talk of the devil, the biggest antlers I've seen this season are moving in those bushes on the hill. Uncas, take your bow and kill that buck for our dinner."

Uncas approached the animal cautiously. "Twang!" went his arrow as he hit the deer.

"Done with great Indian skill," said Hawkeye.

"Sh!" whispered the old chief.

"What's the matter, Chingachgook? Do you hear something?" cried Hawkeye.

The Indian pressed his ear to the ground. "Horses of white men are coming," he said. "Hawkeye, they are your brothers. You must speak to them."

The cracking of dry sticks and the trampling of hoofs got closer. Just as Hawkeye looked up, a British officer came into view, guiding his little band along the beaten path.

Uncas Kills a Buck for Dinner.

"Who comes?" demanded Hawkeye, his finger on the trigger of his long rifle.

"We are friends of the king," said the leader who marched forth to meet Hawkeye. "Permit me to introduce myself. My name is Major Duncan Heyward. We have traveled since morning without food, and we are very tired. We trusted an Indian guide to take us to Fort William Henry, but I'm afraid we're lost. Perhaps you could tell us the way."

"Hoot!" shouted Hawkeye. "An Indian guide lost in the woods! That sounds mighty strange to me!"

"Our guide, Le Renard Subtil, was originally from Canada, where he belonged to the Huron tribe, but he is a Mohawk now and our friend," said Heyward gently. "Now, if you will give me directions to the fort, we shall be on our way."

"Before you go, I should like to see this Indian. If he is an Iroquois, I can tell in a minute by his knavish look and by his paint."

Major Heyward Introduces Himself.

Hawkeye peered through the bushes at Le Renard, who was at the rear of the procession. "I wouldn't go another step with that sly old fox," he warned. "The woods are full of Iroquois, and I have a feeling your so-called Mohawk knows all too well where the Iroquois are hiding."

"Are you sure?" asked the shocked Major Heyward.

"Without a doubt. Now you go keep that scoundrel's attention any way you can. Chingachgook and Uncas are Mohicans. They will take care of him."

Hurriedly, Heyward rode over to where the Indian stood leaning silently and sullenly against a tree. "The scout is going to show us where we can spend the night," he told him.

Le Renard glared at the major. "Then I will go. The pale-faces do not need me. They will see none but their own color."

"And what will you tell the chief at William Henry? That you left his daughters without

Hawkeye Suspects Le Renard Subtil.

a guide?" cried Heyward.

"Though the colonel has a loud voice and long arm, he cannot reach me in the woods."

"I thought we were friends," Heyward said. "I expect you to continue as our guide. When the ladies are rested, we will proceed."

"The pale-faces make themselves slaves to their women," muttered the Indian.

"We must be moving before the sun rises," Heyward told him, "or Montcalm may prevent us from reaching our destination. Now, let me see. Perhaps there is something among my provisions that will whet your appetite."

As the major handed over his pack, the runner uttered a piercing cry and plunged into the bushes. Immediately, Chingachgook and Uncas leaped from their hiding place after him. Their primitive yells, released now in the heat of fury, resounded throughout the forest. Hawkeye fired his rifle into the darkening sky, and the chase was on!

Le Renard Plunges into the Bushes.

The Searchers Return Empty-Handed.

CHAPTER 3

Terror Stalks the Travelers

Major Heyward was too stunned to move. By the time he had collected himself and dashed into the bushes, he met Hawkeye and the two Mohicans returning empty-handed.

"Why have you given up so soon?" the major exclaimed. "We are not safe yet."

"He was just too fast for us," answered Hawkeye breathlessly. "He brushed over the leaves like a snake. But I wounded him."

"That means we are four able bodies against one wounded man!" cried the major.

"Look," said Hawkeye, "you wouldn't get any distance at all before that red devil and his whole pack would be upon you. We'd better get moving, or our scalps will be drying in front of Montcalm's tent tomorrow."

"Then don't desert us," said Heyward. "Defend the ladies and guide us to the fort. Then you can name your own reward."

"The Mohicans and I accept the mission gladly, but we wish no reward," said Hawkeye. "But you must agree to two conditions. First, you must promise to be as quiet as possible. And second, you must promise never to reveal the place where we shall take you."

"I can assure you we will keep our part of the bargain," said Heyward.

"Then follow me, for we are losing precious time," said Hawkeye.

Hawkeye immediately ran to a clump of bushes near the river and pulled a canoe out from its hiding place. He helped the women and the singing master get comfortably seated, then together, he and Heyward walked along the shore, guiding the fragile craft

Boarding Hawkeye's Canoe

upstream. Uncas and Chingachgook, meanwhile, led the horses into hiding.

The two Mohicans rejoined the party at a bend where the river ran between high, jagged rocks covered by tall pine trees. For a brief time, this beautiful, secluded setting gave the sisters a feeling of security. Then Hawkeye, the Indians, and the major jumped into the canoe. Placing his pole against a rock, Hawkeye pushed the canoe directly into the middle of the turbulent current.

Forbidden to stir and almost afraid to breathe lest they should tip over, the passengers watched in mounting suspense. Twenty times they thought the whirling current was sweeping them to destruction. Yet, twenty times Hawkeye's skill brought them through the rapids. At last, the canoe floated gracefully over to the side of a flat rock.

"Where are we?" demanded Heyward.

"You are on an island at the foot of Glenn's Falls," Hawkeye answered. "Now help your

A Terrifying Trip in the Whirling Current

party up on the rock, and the Mohicans and I will bring the provisions."

Once everyone was on shore, Hawkeye and Chingachgook lit torches and led the group into a cavern on the side of the mountain. The cavern was connected to a second one by a narrow tunnel. Once inside, the group relaxed for the first time and began preparations for dinner.

"Come, friend," said Hawkeye, drawing out a keg and addressing the singing master who sat beside him. "Let us drink to friendship. What is your name?"

"David Gamut," replied the singing master.

"A very good name and one handed down from honest forefathers, I'm sure. What is your calling in life?"

"I teach music to young people."

"You might be better employed," said Hawkeye. "Our youngsters go singing and laughing through the woods too much already when they should be silent. Well, I

Heading to a Mountain Cavern

suppose it's your gift and mustn't be denied. Will you lead us in an evening psalm?"

"What could be more fitting after the dangers we faced today!" said David, adjusting his iron-rimmed spectacles.

As he sang the first stanzas of a familiar hymn, the others joined in, one by one, until their voices filled every nook and cranny of the cave. Even Hawkeye was taken back to thoughts of his boyhood when he had first heard the hymn. And hot tears flowed from eyes that had long been hard and dry.

For a while, everyone's spirits lifted. But later as the two young women curled up in the bed of sassafras branches Heyward had made for them, Cora confided, "I won't sleep a wink tonight, Duncan. I just know that somewhere out there in those woods the Iroquois are waiting to murder us all."

"You are perfectly safe as long as you stay inside the cave," Heyward assured her. "And what's more, you have three experienced

David Gamut Leads an Evening Hymn.

woodsmen as your guards."

Hawkeye and the Mohicans kept watch at the entrance to the cave all during the long, uneventful night. However, as the first streaks of dawn appeared over the tree tops, their worst fears were realized.

Dreaded war-whoops filled the air as the Iroquois charged up from the shore. David Gamut, who had insisted on sleeping outside on a rock, became a perfect target. He was wounded by the first burst of Iroquois rifles. Hawkeye leaped to the rock, and several shots from his rifle sent the Indians retreating down the hill.

He and Uncas quickly carried their fallen comrade into the cave. "He shall recover, ladies, and be a wiser man for the ordeal. Take good care of him!" yelled Hawkeye, as he dashed into a nearby thicket with Heyward and Uncas to patrol the shore.

"Perhaps we put up such a good fight that they won't return," Heyward said hopefully.

A Perfect Target for Iroquois Rifles

"You don't know much about this tribe if you think they will give up without taking a single scalp," Hawkeye replied. "If there was one red man, there were forty. And they know exactly how many of us there are too. No, they won't give up. For all we know they may be waiting down by the river for us."

Heyward parted the pine branches and, to his horror, saw four heads peering above the driftwood that had lodged in some rocks. "I see them! I see them!" he cried.

"They are getting ready to rush us," said Hawkeye. "Let them. I promise you the first man who attacks me will meet his death. How I wish it were that French dog, Montcalm!"

At that moment, the four savages sprang from their hiding place, uttering the wildest cries Heyward had ever heard. Hawkeye immediately shot their leader.

"Now, Uncas!" yelled Hawkeye, drawing his knife. "Let's take the rest of them!"

"I See Them! I See Them!"

Uncas obeyed immediately, and his knife downed one Iroquois.

Suddenly, Hawkeye found himself locked in hand to hand combat with a gigantic Indian. Hawkeye and his attacker struggled long and hard for possession of their knives. Finally, the white man's strength proved too much for the Indian, and Hawkeye plunged his knife deep into the red man's heart.

In the meantime, Heyward was involved in his own struggle with an Indian. It was a vicious contest to see who could throw the other over the dizzy height of the cliff. Little by little, they crept nearer the edge, staring each other in the eye every step of the way. For one long moment that seemed like an eternity to the major, the evil smile of the Iroquois flashed before him. Then Heyward felt tough, muscular hands grasp his throat and tighten in a strangle hold. And there on the edge of the cliff, with the water swirling below, Duncan Heyward fought for his life.

Heyward Fights For His Life.

The Iroquois Falls to His Death.

CHAPTER 4

Betrayed!

As the two men swayed dangerously on the rocky ledge, Uncas rushed forward. With a downward thrust of his knife, he slashed the wrists of the Iroquois. As his blood flowed freely, the Iroquois let out one long, blood-curdling scream, then fell over the rocky cliff to his death. Uncas, meanwhile, pulled Heyward back onto safe ground.

"Uncas, you saved my life today. I shall always be deeply indebted to you," said Major Heyward after he had composed himself.

The young Mohican and the British officer shook hands solemnly to solidify the strong bond of friendship that had sprung up between them.

"Saving a friend's life is an obligation in the wilderness," said Hawkeye. "Why, Uncas has stood between me and death five times that I remember, and. . . ."

His statement was interrupted by savage yells that came from the woods.

"Quick, Uncas!" cried Hawkeye. "I'm out of gunpowder. There's more in the canoe."

The young Mohican ran down towards the shore. Within moments, he uttered a loud, piercing cry. The two women ran out of the cave, and the whole party rushed down to the shore. Their canoe, piloted by an Iroquois, was floating straight toward the swift current. The sly thief waved his arm in the air and gave a triumphant victory cry.

"We're too late!" Hawkeye exclaimed bitterly, looking down at his empty rifle.

"What will become of us?" cried Duncan. "Our powder is gone. Our canoe is gone, and

A Sly Thief Steals the Canoe.

you can be sure our enemies will return."

"We will die as bravely as we fought!" cried Hawkeye.

Cora, who had remained silent up to now, suddenly stepped forward. "Why die at all!" she stated firmly. "You brave men must go. You can get through the Iroquois without us. We owe you too much already."

"The Iroquois would never let us travel through the forest," replied Hawkeye. "But we do have a chance, just one—the river!"

"Then, you must take it—by yourselves," cried Cora. "Why should you stay here to be murdered?"

"No!" thundered Hawkeye. "I have a conscience. How could I ever face your father knowing that I had abandoned you?"

"Then you must send him to rescue us. It is our only hope."

Hawkeye thought about Cora's words for several moments. "Uncas! Chingachgook! Did you hear what she said?" he cried. "It makes

Cora Urges the Men to Go On.

sense, don't you think?"

"Good!" muttered Chingachgook. Then, in one quick step, he bounded to the edge of the rock and dropped silently into the water.

"You have spoken wisely," Hawkeye told Cora. "You must believe that our mission will be successful, but if you are captured, break twigs on bushes along your path and know that you have a friend who will follow you to the ends of the earth."

Then, casting aside their rifles, Hawkeye and Uncas plunged into the murky depths of the Hudson River. After a moment, they emerged down near the rapids.

"You must go with them, Duncan," Cora said with a quivering lip.

"Is that all the faith you have in me as your protector?" Heyward demanded angrily.

"There is nothing more you can do here," she said, "and there are others who need you. The worst thing that can befall us is death."

"There are some things worse than death,"

Chingachgook Drops into the Water.

he answered in a hoarse voice. Then he looked wistfully at the beautiful Alice who stood before him. "One of them would be to leave you. Whatever happens, we shall face it together." With that, he wrapped Alice's shawl around her shoulders, then led the two women back into the cave.

Now that he had assumed the full position of leadership, Major Heyward made a valiant attempt to calm his group and reassure them their rescue was just a matter of time.

The two sisters huddled in a corner near David Gamut, who had recovered sufficiently to lead them in singing. In the meantime, Heyward was busy concealing the cave entrance with sassafras branches. Then, clutching his pistol, he sat down in the center of the room to listen for signs of trouble.

He didn't have long to wait. When the first piercing yell reached the cavern, Heyward's heart leaped into his throat, and Alice threw herself in her sister's arms, sobbing, "We are

Heyward Reassures His Group.

lost!"

"We're not lost yet," said Heyward calmly. "Those shouts came from the center of the island. We haven't been discovered. There is still hope."

The words were hardly out of his mouth when screams and cries spread around them in every direction. Some of the savages' calls from the water's edge were answered by other Indians posted above the cavern. Still others howled fiercely as they trooped into the adjoining cavern.

In the midst of this tumult, a victorious yell was raised just down the hill from the hidden entrance to the cave. At first, Heyward thought they had been detected, but then he realized it was the discovery of Hawkeye's rifle that was causing all the excitement.

"La Longue Carabine!" the savages cried over and over again, as if the trophy were a symbol of its owner's death.

"La Longue Carabine!"

"What are they saying?" asked Cora.

"The long rifle," said Heyward who understood French. "That's their name for Hawkeye. They found the rifle, but not him. That means he's escaped and is still alive."

The savages continued their search for the famous scout in the adjoining cave, looking futilely through the leaves and debris. They did not notice the little tunnel connecting the two caverns, for it was piled high with the leaves and branches the women had used for a bed. Satisfied that neither Hawkeye nor his party were to be found, the savages fled back down the steep embankment.

"They are gone," said the major, breathing easier. "At last we are safe!"

"Let us give thanks to God," Alice said emotionally. But as she spoke, the words froze in her mouth. She fell back in horror.

Heyward turned and peered out through an opening at the top of the cavern. There, he beheld the fierce, wicked features of their

The Savages Search the Adjoining Cave.

former guide, Le Renard Subtil. The major ducked, hoping that the Indian's eyes, accustomed to the outside, had not yet focused in the dark and detected them. However, it was too late. They had been betrayed by the guide!

Heyward was enraged at the look of brutal victory on the traitor's face. Without thinking, he foolishly took aim and fired his pistol through the opening. But the Indian merely slipped around the side of the cave and, with ear-shattering war-whoops, summoned his companions back up the hill.

Before Heyward had time to recover from the shock, his weak barrier of branches was thrown aside. From the tunnel and from the opening, the red men rushed into the cave. They dragged Heyward, Gamut, and the terrified women out into the bright sunlight. There, the prisoners stood surrounded on all sides by the whole band of leering, triumphant Iroquois.

Discovered!

Curious About Their Prisoners

CHAPTER 5

Le Renard Subtil Seeks Revenge

In wide-eyed, childlike amazement, the warriors swarmed around their prisoners. They lifted the iron-rimmed spectacles from David's nose and looked quizzically through his hymn book. They even fingered the material of his sky-blue coat, of Hayward's uniform, and of the women's wrinkled clothing. They toyed mischievously with Alice's long blonde hair which was unlike anything they had ever seen before.

"La Longue Carabine," they wailed repeatedly as they circled around the two white men.

"What do they want?" Heyward asked Le Renard Subtil, trying to hide his contempt for the man who had deceived him.

"They ask for the hunter who knows the paths through the woods and who shot me with his long rifle," he answered, placing his hands on the leaves that bandaged his shoulder wound. "If we don't find him, we will have the blood of those that hide him."

"Hawkeye and the Mohicans have gone," Heyward told him with a satisfied smile.

The news of Hawkeye's escape sent the red men into a frenzy. They quickly tied their captives' hands behind their backs and led them down to the shore. There, they mounted some horses that were waiting in the brush.

Realizing the grimness of their situation, Heyward tried to bribe Le Renard by appealing to his vanity and greed. "What a great chief you have become!" he said slyly as he rode alongside him. "If you were wise enough to trick me, then you should be able to see

The Captives Are Led Down to the Shore.

the benefits of delivering the Munro sisters safely to Fort William Henry. Their father will reward you with bags of gold, much fine powder, and many long rifles. This should mean more to you than the life of one scout."

"Enough talk," said Le Renard, charging ahead. "You will see what I decide in good time."

They proceeded in silence southward, following a road in the opposite direction from the fort. With the sun as his only guide, Le Renard plowed through the wilderness for several hours before he stopped his caravan to rest. While his Iroquois comrades gorged themselves on the raw meat of a deer they had slain, he sat alone, lost in thought.

Finally, he walked over to where Cora sat resting on a tree stump. "I want to talk to the daughter of Munro," he said.

"What is it you wish to say?" she asked, knowing full well that her presence of mind might save all their lives.

Plowing Through the Wilderness

"Listen," said the Indian, "I was once an Iroquois chief on the Great Lakes. I was happy until the pale-faces came into my woods and gave me the fire-water that made me evil."

"Yes, I have heard something about this."

"Did you hear that it was your father who caused my greatest disgrace? He made a law saying that the red man who drank fire-water and did damage to the white man's cabins should be punished. It was he who tied me to the stake and whipped me like a dog!"

"He was only seeing that justice was done!"

"How can that be justice? I was not myself at the time. It was the fire-water that acted for me. But I shall remember it forever."

"If my father has done you an injustice, show him how an Indian can forgive and take us back to him. He will reward you with gold."

"No!" Le Renard cried, shaking his head. "It is not gold I want, but revenge!"

"Then take your revenge out on me," Cora

Le Renard Was Whipped Like a Dog.

pleaded, "and let the others go."

Le Renard stared the beautiful woman straight in the eye as he spoke. "I will do what you ask if you will come live in my wigwam forever."

Although she was revolted by such a proposal of marriage, Cora hid her disgust and maintained sufficient self-control to reply, "What pleasure would you have with a woman of another race whom you don't love? It would be better to take my father's gold to buy gifts for an Iroquois maiden."

"No," he yelled, "it is the daughter of Munro that I want—for *revenge!*"

"Monster!" Cora screamed. "None but a fiend could plan such vengeance!"

The Indian answered her defiance by summoning his comrades to his side. "Revenge! Revenge!" he whooped as they tied the terrified prisoners to the trees and splintered long strips of pine to ram into their flesh.

"Now, what do you say?" asked Le Renard,

A Marriage Proposal for Revenge!

taunting Cora as she stood tied helplessly to a tree. "Your head was too good for the pillow in my wigwam. How will you feel when it rolls on the ground and becomes a plaything for the wolves?" He stopped and leered cruelly at her. "It's not too late to change your mind. If you do, I shall give the others their freedom."

"What did he say?" asked Alice.

"He promises to release all of you if I will become his wife," said Cora, sobbing. "Oh, Duncan! Oh, Alice! Tell me what I should do. Is life to be purchased at such a sacrifice?"

"No, Cora!" cried Heyward. "The thought itself is worse than a thousand deaths."

"It would be better to die as we have lived, together!" wept Alice.

"Then die!" shouted Le Renard, hurling his tomahawk at Alice. It landed in the tree just above her head and quivered there. "Die! Die! The daughters of Munro shall die before the sun sinks in the western sky!"

"The Daughters of Munro Shall Die!"

A Rifle Shot Saves Heyward.

CHAPTER 6

Hawkeye Comes to the Rescue

The sight of Cora and Alice tied to the trees, helpless in the hands of their tormentors, nearly drove Duncan Heyward mad. Furiously, he disentangled himself from the twigs that bound him and leaped upon an Indian who was poised for the final attack against the women.

At first, the two men grappled and fell to the ground. But then the Iroquois rose and, with the weight of a giant, pinned the major to the ground. Heyward saw a knife gleaming inches above him. Then suddenly the crack of a rifle sounded through the trees. With a thud, the Indian fell dead beside him.

"La Longue Carabine!" cried the Iroquois as Hawkeye and the Mohicans dashed from the brush to interrupt the massacre that had been intended for their friends. Blow after furious blow fell, and soon four of the red men lay dead under the stately pines.

While the rest of his warriors were still fighting, one of the Iroquois cut Cora loose from the tree and threw her to her knees. Jerking her head back, he ran his knife around her soft, ivory neck, laughing hysterically. Uncas jumped upon the savage and pulled him some yards away from the terrified woman. Then he plunged his knife into the Iroquois' heart.

Meanwhile, Chingachgook and Le Renard were involved in a frantic struggle of their own. Le Renard was on the ground, and just as the Mohican was preparing to strike the death blow, Le Renard rolled swiftly away, leaped to his feet, and bounded like a deer

A Moment of Terror!

into the forest.

"Let him go," cried Hawkeye. "He is but one man. Now he is separated from his French friends, and he has no rifle. He is as harmless as a rattlesnake who has lost his fangs."

"Yes, let him go," pleaded Alice. "All that matters is we are safe. Hawkeye, we will be eternally grateful to you for saving us."

"We will, indeed," added the major. "Now, Hawkeye, tell us of your adventures since you left the cave and dove into the river."

"Well, instead of going to the fort, which we could never have done in time to rescue you, we swam down the river and hid along the bank. We heard your capture and saw your departure into the woods."

"It is a miracle you found us," said David Gamut, "because there were two groups, each moving in a different direction."

"Ay! That threw us off the track for a while, but then Uncas found a lady's glove and a

Uncas Found a Lady's Glove.

trail of broken bushes that led us to this spot. Now that we're all together again, I think we had best get started on the road to Fort William Henry."

"Yes," agreed Heyward, motioning to his group. "The sun is already low over those far distant mountains."

The party rode until sunset, when Hawkeye led them into a dense thicket of chestnut trees. "Here is where we will camp for the night," he said, pointing to an old blockhouse that nestled in the trees, crumbling and forgotten. The roof of this observation post had long since fallen off, and only three walls remained standing.

Protectively, Heyward held the sisters back, while Hawkeye and the Mohicans examined the ruins with great curiosity. For, as Chingachgook told them, a great battle had been fought here years ago between the Mohicans and the Mohawks.

After inspecting the ruins, Hawkeye and

"We Will Camp for the Night."

the Mohicans cleared the leaves out of a spring and uncovered a fountain of pure, crystal clear water for the weary travelers to drink. Hawkeye and Uncas then covered the roof of the blockhouse with shrubs and made a soft bed of dried leaves in one corner for the sisters to sleep on.

A determined Heyward kept watch outside the house way into the wee hours of the morning. He sat perfectly still, listening to the gentle breathing of the sisters and watching the stars twinkle through the trees. The last thing he remembered before drifting off to sleep was the mournful notes of a whippoorwill blending with the hoots of an owl. However, he had been asleep only a short time when a light tap on his shoulder awakened him.

"Who goes there?" he asked, jumping up and reaching for his sword. "Speak up! Are you friend or foe?"

"Friend," replied Chingachgook in a low

Heyward Keeps Watch.

voice. "The moon comes, and the white man's fort is far off. It is time to move, for now sleep shuts the eyes of the Frenchmen."

"You are right, Chingachgook. I will get my companions ready to travel."

With scarcely a backward glance at the little shelter silhouetted against the chestnuts, they trotted down the moonlit path that led toward Lake George. After an hour's travel, the tops of the mountains loomed ahead.

"How far are we from the fort now?" asked David Gamut.

"We still have a long way to go," Hawkeye told him, "and it won't be easy getting through with the French entrenched around the fort. Nor is there much time left if we are to slip in under cover of darkness."

"How do you suggest we go about it?" inquired Heyward.

"There is only one way," Hawkeye explained. "We must climb that mountain you see to the west and come down around the

"We Must Climb That Mountain."

shore where the fort is situated. We will have to dodge the French guards and pray to God to see us through. Now, let's be off!"

They struck out across the valley and crossed the rocky terrain that led to the foot of the mountain. Slowly but surely, they plodded up the steep hill to the cone-shaped summit. As they all joined forces again, they saw the first hint of dawn come blushing up over ragged tree tops.

The mountain on which they stood was part of a chain that extended far into Canada. Below them lay the glittering waters of Lake George and on its western shore, Fort William Henry. From where they stood, they could see the smoke rising from Montcalm's camp, where ten thousand Frenchmen were waiting to attack Colonel Munro's forces. The first roar of artillery rose from the valley and thundered through the hills.

"That shot was aimed at William Henry," said Hawkeye. "Look! The fog is moving in

Fort William Henry and Montcalm's Camp

from the lake. It will make a perfect cover. Now, if you are up to it, we must push on."

"We are ready," cried Cora.

"How I wish I had a thousand men who feared death as little as you!" said Hawkeye as he proceeded down the steep incline.

As they approached the woods that lay outside the gates of the fort, the fog suddenly began to roll in from the lake and swirl around them.

"Qui va la?" called a voice from the mist. "Who goes there?"

"What was that?" asked David Gamut.

But there was no time for an answer. The call was repeated by a dozen other French voices. Muskets exploded on every side of them, and the order to advance was heard.

"Cora! Alice! Stay close to me," called Major Heyward. But in the thick fog, the Munro sisters were nowhere to be seen. And somewhere in that fog, marching toward the terrified party, was the whole French army!

Searching in the Thick Fog

Munro Orders the Gates Open.

CHAPTER 7

Munro Makes a Hard Decision

Above the haze and roar of the French invasion, the booming voice of a Scotsman rang out. "Stand firm, men. Hold your fire until you see the enemy."

"Father! Father!" came a cry from the mist. "It is I, Alice. Over here. Come save us!"

"Praise be to God!" Colonel Munro answered. "My children are safe at last!" Turning to his lieutenant he said, "Stop all shooting lest you kill my daughters. Throw open the gates and let me out. Then we will drive off these French dogs."

Heyward heard the rusty hinges creak as

the gates of Fort William Henry swung open. He saw a long line of soldiers pour forth to attack the French. Then, as the mist parted, a welcome sight greeted him. Almost instantly the Munro sisters were cradled in their father's arms, tearfully enjoying every moment of their happy reunion.

"I'm very grateful to you, Duncan," said Colonel Munro, shaking the hand of his old friend. "You have guided my daughters bravely through the wilderness on a perilous journey."

"It's Hawkeye here and these Mohicans to whom you owe your thanks," Heyward told him as the rest of the party joined them. "They have saved our lives more than once."

"Then come into the fort," said the colonel, motioning toward the English stronghold. "There's venison on the spit and cornbread aplenty. Come eat. You must be starving."

The joy of the reunion was short-lived, however. As the days of the siege passed, it

A Happy Reunion

was increasingly obvious that Munro was in desperate trouble. More than half his guns were out of service, walls were crumbling everywhere, and provisions were running low. Although badly outnumbered, the English fought bravely. But their losses kept mounting. Each day they lived on the hope that reinforcements would arrive.

On the fifth day, when there was still no sign of them, a brief truce was declared. Major Heyward met with General Montcalm, who gave him a message to deliver to Munro.

The colonel was alone in his quarters when Heyward arrived back at the fort. Instead of demanding to know the results of the major's mission, Munro was pacing the door, lost in thought when Heyward entered the room.

"I have a message from the Marquis of Montcalm, sir," said Heyward.

"Let that Frenchman go to the devil!" exclaimed the colonel. "He is not master of William Henry yet, nor will he ever be,

Heyward Meets with Montcalm.

provided Webb sends us the men we need. No, Heyward, there is another urgent matter to discuss. It concerns your feelings for Cora."

"But, sir," said Heyward, "it is not Cora, but Alice whom I wish to marry."

Colonel Munro resumed his pacing. After several minutes, he began to speak softly. "There are some things I must tell you about our family."

Each drew up a chair, and for a moment the French and Indian War and Montcalm's message were forgotten.

"Years ago in Scotland," Munro began, "I was engaged to Alice Graham, but her father opposed our marriage because I was penniless. So I sought my fortune in the West Indies, where I married another lady, Cora's mother. She was a descendant of slaves, but I loved her very much. She died shortly after Cora was born, and I returned to Scotland with my daughter to find that Alice had waited for me all those years.

An Urgent Matter To Discuss

"I finally married Alice, but she died giving birth to my daughter you now wish to marry." Tears rolled down his cheeks as he remembered the tragedy. At length, he pulled himself together and, in his best military tone, he said, "Now, Major Heyward, let's hear that message from Montcalm."

"He is anxious to meet with you as soon as it can be arranged," said Heyward.

"Then arrange it, my boy," cried Munro, banging on his desk. "Arrange it."

A few hours later, the two military leaders rode cautiously out to the middle of a plain, each with an aide carrying the white flag of truce. In addition to his officers, the French leader was surrounded by a swarthy band of Iroquois chiefs and warriors from their tribes. Heyward stopped short, and his blood ran cold as he saw among them the sinister face of his enemy, Le Renard Subtil. As their eyes met, the Indian turned and disappeared into the crowd.

Two Leaders Meet Under Flags of Truce.

Being the superior officer, Montcalm was the first to speak. "Monsieur, would you like to tour my camp and see for yourself the impossibility of resisting my large numbers?"

"General Webb has enough troops to replenish our ranks," answered Munro confidently.

"Fortunately for us, they are not on hand, nor are they likely to be. You will see that when you read this letter which we intercepted on its way to you."

Colonel Munro seized the letter and, as he read its contents, a look of horror spread over his face. "Webb has betrayed me!" he said bitterly. "He writes that he can send no more men and urges our surrender."

"No!" cried Heyward. "We are still masters of the fort and of our honor. Let us go back and fight till our death."

"Wait," cried Montcalm, "you haven't heard my terms yet. Why risk all your lives for a lost cause? I will grant you an honorable

Horrifying News!

surrender. You may keep your flags, your arms, and your lives. You must give up the fort at dawn tomorrow, for I must destroy it."

Colonel Munro gave the matter his complete concentration and finally ordered Heyward to prepare the treaty of surrender. "I have lived to see two things in my old age that I never expected," he said, "an Englishman like Webb afraid to support a friend—and a brave Frenchman too honest to profit by his advantage." Turning quickly, the broken-hearted leader directed his horse back to his fort on the lake.

All was quiet in both camps during the night of August 9, 1757. Just before dawn, Montcalm slipped from his tent, throwing his cloak over his shoulders, partly as a disguise and partly for protection against the cool night air. He passed his guard with the customary salute and hurried in the direction of William Henry.

He gave the correct passwords to all the

Montcalm Leaves His Tent.

French sentries and soon reached that side of the fort which touched on Lake George. Leaning back against a tree, he studied the dark shadows of the English fort. Satisfied that all was in order and that there would be no surprise attack by the English at dawn, he started to leave. Suddenly, he saw Colonel Munro approach the edge of the ramparts. The British officer stood gazing at the approaching dawn over the glassy waters of the lake.

Not wishing to be noticed, the Frenchman started to slip away quietly. But as he turned, he heard a strange movement on the lake. A dark figure rose from the water and walked silently onto land within a few feet of where General Montcalm was concealed.

"Le Renard Subtil!" gasped Montcalm.

Then, before he knew what was happening, Montcalm saw the Indian lift his rifle and aim directly at the silhouette of Colonel Munro.

An Attempted Murder!

Montcalm Disarms Le Renard.

CHAPTER 8

The Massacre at William Henry

For a moment, Montcalm stood frozen in his hiding place. Then, with his cloak flying wildly behind him, he dashed forward and shoved the barrel of Le Renard's rifle toward the ground. Grabbing the Indian by the shoulder, he pulled him back into the trees.

"What is the meaning of this?" Montcalm cried in exasperation. "Don't you know the hatchet is buried between the English and the French?"

"The pale-faces make friends now," answered the redskin, "and not one of my warriors has a scalp."

"That doesn't matter," Montcalm retorted. "You are pledged not to attack the friends of France."

"I am a great chief," Le Renard cried. "I will have my revenge for the marks Munro left on me. You will see!" With that, he whirled and ran back toward the Iroquois encampment.

There was a frown on Montcalm's face as he, too, retraced his steps back to his tent and roused his men to action. Soon the valley echoed with the marching music of the French grenadiers as they began their procession to William Henry at dawn.

The change of command took place with dignity and decorum. The English and Americans made a brave attempt to conceal their wounded pride as the French flag was raised high above the fort. And the French, on their part, refrained from any behavior that might have been interpreted as taunting or condescending.

The French Flag Is Raised Above the Fort.

But Colonel Munro's grief was apparent to all. Stern and proud, he led his columns out the gates, giving up his last claim on the fort. Heyward and the women and children followed behind, while the wounded brought up the rear.

Along the sweeping borders of the forest hung a dark cloud of Iroquois. They eyed the passage of their enemies like hovering vultures who were kept from swooping upon their prey by the presence of the French. However, when the colorful shawl of one of the English women attracted the eyes of a wild Iroquois, he went to grab it, and trouble erupted.

"Let him have it!" Cora cried as the woman pulled her shawl closer, but the advice came too late. In a violent fit of rage, the Indian raised his tomahawk and killed the woman and the child she was clutching in her arms.

At that instant, Le Renard placed his hand over his mouth and began a series of war-

Trouble Erupts.

whoops that drew a seemingly endless stream of thousands of savages from the forest. Tomahawks and knives flew in every direction, and screams and yells resounded from one end of the plain to the other. Death was everywhere as the Indians slaughtered men, women, and children in their path.

Cora, standing riveted to the spot, waved in vain to her father who streaked by her in his fruitless search for Montcalm. At her feet lay the unconscious form of her sister. Just as she and David Gamut stooped to revive Alice, the shadow of a sinister intruder fell over them.

"Le Renard!" cried Cora, looking up.

"My wigwam is still open," he said, fingering her dress with his dirty hands. "Is it not better than this place?" He laughed loudly as he held up his blood-stained hands.

"Monster!" she shrieked. "You and you alone are responsible for starting this bloody massacre!"

Le Renard's Bloody Massacre!

Le Renard ignored her remark. "Are you ready now to travel to my village?"

"Never! Never!" she cried, backing away from him in horror.

As she spoke, the Iroquois scooped up Alice's limp body and headed toward the forest. Unwilling to abandon Alice without a struggle, Cora and David flew after him, making their way through the wounded and dead on the plain.

When they reached the first pine grove, Le Renard caught Cora in his arms and carried her, kicking and screaming, to his horse. Forcing her to mount and ride behind the unconscious Alice, he led his horse deep into the forest. David Gamut, huffing and puffing, followed behind them.

It was not until several hours later that Colonel Munro and Heyward, aided by Hawk-eye and the Mohicans, were able to begin the search for Cora and Alice. It was Uncas who actually led them to the pine grove where

An Unwilling Bride

they discovered Cora's riding veil dangling from a limb.

"What does this mean?" asked Munro wildly, as he crushed the veil in his hands. "What has happened to my daughters?"

"Well, if they have gone alone, they are quite likely moving in a circle nearby. But if the Iroquois have captured them, then they are probably heading for the Canadian border," Hawkeye explained grimly.

"Look! Over here!" interrupted Chingachgook. "Here are the prints of Le Renard's moccasins."

"And here is David Gamut's pitch pipe," yelled Heyward, pulling the object out of a brier patch. "Thank God he stayed with them. But where is Alice?"

"I'm afraid there is no sign of her yet," answered Hawkeye. "But never fear, sir, we will not give up."

An excited cry from Uncas, kneeling beneath a fir tree, brought the whole party

Cora's Riding Veil Is Discovered.

running. The Mohican rose to his feet and held up a ruby pendant that glittered brightly in the late afternoon sun.

"It's Alice's," Heyward exclaimed as he, grabbed it and held it against his heart. "I remember seeing it around her neck when she rode out this morning."

"There's no doubt about it then," Hawkeye told Munro and Heyward. "They have been carried into captivity by Le Renard Subtil."

The old man fell to his knees in agony. "Dear God, have mercy on them!" he wept.

"You must not give up hope," said Hawkeye, putting his arm around the colonel's shoulder. "Being captured is a far sight better than starving in the wilderness, and they will leave a wide trail for us to follow. Now, I will wager you fifty beaver skins that the Mohicans and I will enter the Iroquois tents before the month is over!"

Uncas Finds Alice's Ruby Pendant.

The Search Party Sets Out.

CHAPTER 9

A Race Against Time

"We cannot start on this expedition without planning," said Hawkeye. "The Indians make their plans over a council fire, and it is a wise thing to do. We must return to the fort tonight, and tomorrow we will be fresh and ready to start."

Heyward and Munro would have preferred to leave immediately, but they bowed to the scout's wisdom and slept briefly.

The heavens were still studded with stars when they slipped into a birch canoe and headed silently across Lake George toward the Iroquois lands that lay to the north.

As the day dawned, they passed through a narrow channel and stole cautiously among the hundreds of little islands that dotted this portion of the lake. It was by this route that Montcalm had traveled with his army, and the search party feared he might well have left some Indians behind to ambush stragglers.

At the opening of an intricate channel, Chingachgook signaled for them all to be quiet. His eyes moved warily from island to island on both sides of them

"What's the matter?" inquired Hawkeye.

The Indian gravely raised his paddle and pointed to a small wooded island that lay before them. "Smoke," he announced. "It comes from a fire that burns low."

"Push on, men!" ordered Hawkeye. "Push with all your might!"

The whole party paddled furiously, but moments later, the crack of a rifle told them that they had been discovered. Over their

Smoke Means Danger Ahead.

shoulders, they saw a stream of savages flock to their canoes and push off from the sandy shore. Their even paddle strokes soon brought their canoe within two hundred yards of Hawkeye's canoe. His long rifle was aimed.

But a cry from Uncas caused Hawkeye to look at the long, low island looming before them. From its shore, another war canoe was heading towards them.

Soon, a barrage of bullets was coming fast and furiously from every direction. Hawkeye, alarmed at this new danger, suddenly took aim and fired, killing the captain of the first canoe. With one long, agonizing cry, the Indian dropped his rifle into the water and fell back into his comrades' arms.

Cooly and calmly, the search party shot ahead until the savages were forced to retreat. Soon the Indians were only specks on the horizon.

The route Hawkeye's party was taking lay

Hawkeye's Bullet Finds Its Mark.

along a wide stretch of water that was lined by high, ragged mountains. The strokes of their paddles grew more even, and for the first time after their narrow escape, they began to relax.

Several hours later, the canoe glided into a bay near the north end of the lake. They landed there, carried the canoe into the woods, and made camp.

When the sun came up the next morning, it was Uncas who picked up Le Renard's trail on a spot of fresh earth that had recently been upturned by some heavy animals.

"A hound never ran on a more beautiful scent," Hawkeye told his companions. Their spirits were high and their hopes raised as they moved out.

The astonishing success of the chase, which had covered more than forty miles, gave the party renewed confidence. Munro and Heyward were amazed at how quickly their scout uncovered the false trails and sudden turns

Uncas Picks Up the Trail.

that their shifty enemy had devised in an attempt to confuse them.

By late afternoon, they arrived at a spot where the captives had apparently spent the night. Burned embers, the remains of a deer, and a small bower for sleeping told the story. Footprints were everywhere, but the trail had mysteriously ended.

A careful search of the area revealed only two stray horses that had been left to roam.

"What does this mean?" asked Heyward.

"It means we are entering enemy country," answered Hawkeye. "If the Iroquois were still fleeing, they would not have let the horses run free. Now we must all band together to find the path to the Iroquois settlement."

The search was renewed in earnest, the men going over the ground inch by inch, turning over every leaf and stone. Soon, a cry from Uncas brought everyone running. He had found a moccasin print in the mud.

"It's not the print of an Indian," said

The Trail Ends Mysteriously.

Hawkeye, looking around the bed of the dam where the impression had been made. "The weight is too much on the heel. David must have been forced to wear moccasins."

"White man went first," Uncas explained.

"Right," agreed Hawkeye, "and Le Renard followed behind, walking in his step."

"But what happened to Cora and Alice?" cried Heyward.

"That sly Iroquois found some tricky way to carry them and throw us off the track," Hawkeye explained. "But do not fear, we shall see their pretty little feet again before many miles go by."

"Perhaps he used this handbarrow," Colonel Munro suggested, picking up the fragments of boughs that were still tied together with willow twigs.

"He's a cunning devil," said Hawkeye, "but the game is not over yet. Look! Now you can see several moccasin prints. Look here!"

"Iroquois wigwams not so far away now,"

A Handbarrow To Carry the Women?

the older Mohican said.

"All right, Chingachgook, you take the hill to the right. Uncas, you follow the brook to the left," said Hawkeye. "The rest of us will continue on the trail. If anything should happen, the signal will be three croaks of a crow."

The Indians went their separate ways, while Hawkeye and the Englishmen marched into a little thicket where the path ended for the second time. Peering through the trees, they saw a small lake whose peaceful surface was disturbed only by the occasional plunge of a beaver. Situated on its banks in neat rows were the earthen dwellings of the Iroquois nation.

Hawkeye was all ready to give the crow's call when a rustling in the leaves distracted him. Just ahead, a strange Indian, crawling on all fours, came into view. He, too, seemed occupied in observing the village.

It was hard to tell much about his features

Finding the Iroquois Village

because his face was smeared with a grotesque mask of war-paint. And like all Iroquois, his head was shaved except for a tuft down the middle. Three faded hawk feathers dangled loosely from his tuft of hair. A ragged calico vest went halfway round his chest. A shirt had been substituted for pants, with his legs fitting into the arm openings, and deerskin moccasins covered his cut feet. This was an individual of miserable appearance.

Little by little, Hawkeye crept through the underbrush until he was only a few yards away from his enemy. Suddenly, the red man stood up, completely fearless, and faced him eye to eye. Hawkeye burst out in a fit of silent laughter.

Both Colonel Munro and Major Heyward fell back in amazement, thunderstruck, unable to speak. Finally, Hawkeye spoke for, them.

"David! David Gamut!" he exclaimed. "Whatever are you doing in that outfit?"

A Fearless Red Man?

"The Iroquois Dressed Me As One of Them."

CHAPTER 10

Heyward Plays a Dangerous Game

"Actually, I'm a lucky fellow," the singing master said, spinning around so that his old friends could get a close look at him. "The Iroquois have been so fascinated by my singing that they dressed me as one of them and let me come and go as I please."

Hawkeye threw back his head and roared with laughter. The thought of scrawny David Gamut prowling these woods disguised as a fierce Indian warrior was amusing indeed.

However, David's reaction was far from humorous. Fighting back the tears, he shook hands warmly all around. "I was beginning to think I'd never see you good people again," he said.

"Naturally, we're glad to see that you are safe," said the distraught Colonel Munro. "But tell me, what has happened to my daughters?"

"Cora has been taken to a neighboring tribe, the Delawares, I believe. All I know for certain is that they are allies of Montcalm, but they were not involved in the massacre at William Henry."

"What about Alice?" asked Major Heyward.

"The Iroquois always separate their prisoners, sir. She is being held captive in the Iroquois village across the lake."

"Then there's not a moment to lose," cried Heyward. "We must set them free as soon as possible."

"It won't be easy," David told them. "Their leader, Le Renard Subtil, is possessed of an evil spirit that no power on earth can tame."

"Where is he now?" asked Hawkeye.

Gamut Reveals Where the Girls Are.

"Away hunting moose."

"Then you must go back, David," the scout said, "and let the sisters know we are here. Our signal to meet again will be the whippoorwill's whistle."

"Wait! Wait!" cried Duncan Heyward. "I'm going with him."

"You!" exclaimed the astonished Hawkeye. "Are you tired of seeing the sun rise and set?"

"Look," Heyward argued, "David is living proof that the Iroquois can be merciful."

"Ay, but he has a special gift that pleases them."

"Then, I, too, will wear a disguise and play a role for these fools. I am going to free Alice or die in the process. My mind is made up."

Hawkeye knew only too well the dangers of such a masquerade, but seeing that Heyward was determined, he finally consented.

Come, major," he said. "Chingachgook has many paints. He will make you look like a

Heyward Wants To Go with Gamut.

fool too. Sit down on this log."

All during the hour-long session, Heyward sat perfectly still while the elder Mohican skillfully painted lines and shadows that transformed him into a medicine man from the Ticonderoga tribe. As Chingachgook stood back to admire his handiwork, the on-lookers applauded appreciatively.

"Surely with your knowledge of French, with your woodsman's clothes, and with all the advice I have pumped into you, you are bound to succeed," Hawkeye said, slapping him on the back.

"God bless you," Colonel Munro whispered as he, Hawkeye, and the two Mohicans watched this strange, adventurous pair make their way past the beavers' pond and into the Iroquois stronghold.

A dozen warriors stood at the doorway of the first lodge as Gamut led Heyward up the hill in the twilight. The redskins stepped aside to allow them to enter. Suddenly, the

Transforming Heyward into a Medicine Man

major found himself standing in the midst of a large council chamber filled with fierce savages. Inwardly, he felt his blood curdle in anger and rage, but he knew he must hide his feelings if he were to save Alice. Imitating David's example, he sat down on a pile of brush and remained silent.

The Indians crowded around him, studying every aspect of his being with great curiosity. At length, one of the elder warriors spoke, but in the language of the Iroquois, which Heyward could not understand.

"Do none of my brothers speak English or French?" he called out in simple French. When there was no answer, he continued, "The King of France would be sad to know that none of his friends in this wise and brave nation can speak his language."

There was a long pause, and finally the old man spoke in French. "When our Great Spirit talks to his people, it is in the Iroquois tongue."

Inside the Council Chamber

"The Great Spirit talks to all people," said Heyward evasively. "He knows no difference in his children whether the color of their skin be red or black or white. The Great Spirit has sent me, a man who practices the art of healing, to inquire if any among you are sick."

There was a low buzz around the room, and Heyward could see the excitement on the faces of the braves. Perhaps all of Hawkeye's coaching would serve him well after all.

Just as the Iroquois spokesman was preparing an answer, a high, shrill yell, like that of a wolf, arose from the forest. All the occupants of the lodge dashed into the dark night to discover the source of the commotion.

Heyward found himself lost in a throng of joyously screaming men, women, and children, all bearing clubs and axes to be used in a brutal native ritual. An Indian brave, a prisoner of a returning war party, was standing at the head of two lines formed by the savage villagers. His punishment was to run the

A Brutal Native Ritual

gauntlet—to run between those two lines of frenzied Iroquois and receive the blows of their clubs, tomahawks, axes, and knives.

When the signal was given, the brave turned, and instead of running the gauntlet, he bolted toward the woods. With loud shouts, his captors tore after him and dragged him back, beating, kicking, and punching him savagely. When he fell to his knees, unable to bear their torture any longer, they dragged him into the council chambers.

Inside, the Indian stood by one of the posts that supported the roof, breathing hard after his struggle, but bravely maintaining his composure. In the dim light, Heyward was unable to distinguish any of his features.

While the council huddled in a corner, deliberating on the fate of their unruly captive, the women teased and taunted him. A wrinkled old hag strutted before him, waving her arms in the air and screaming insults. "Your squaws are the mothers of deer," she said,

The Old Hag Taunts the Prisoner.

cackling loudly, "but if a bear or wildcat were born among you, you would flee in terror."

When the Indian refused to respond, she flew into a rage and began to foam at the mouth. "We shall make you petticoats and find you a husband," she shrieked.

The council had dispersed now. As the elder warrior approached the captive to announce their verdict, the old woman snatched a flaming torch from the wall and shoved it in the youth's face.

He looked quickly away, and for one brief moment the eyes of Heyward and Uncas met and held, although neither man flinched nor changed his expression. Finally, the young Mohican turned back to face his accuser and learn his fate.

Heyward Recognizes Uncas.

"You Have Proved Yourself a Man."

CHAPTER 11

A Daring Scheme Unfolds

Silence reigned in the large council chamber as the gray-haired warrior approached Uncas. "Mohican," he said, "you have proved yourself a man. Rest in peace till morning comes and our men return from hunting your comrades. Then, you shall learn whether you live or die."

Uncas never moved a muscle as he listened to the Iroquois decree. "Do you have no ears?" he asked his captor. "Twice since I've been your prisoner, I've heard the shots of Hawkeye's rifle. Your men will not be back."

The aged chieftain ignored this bold

statement and, with a crook of his finger, motioned Uncas to be seated on the opposite end of the log from Heyward. The two men sat perfectly still, ignoring each other, both fully aware of the consequences if their true relationship were discovered.

The warriors pulled out their pipes now, and as they discussed the success of their most recent war party, they puffed away on the hollow handles. Swirls of white smoke rose slowly, spiraling to the ceiling.

After a while, a second chief put down his pipe and approached the visiting medicine man. "An evil spirit lives in the wife of one of my bravest warriors," he said. "Can the cunning stranger frighten him away?"

"Spirits differ," Heyward answered mysteriously. "Some yield to the power of wisdom, while others are too strong."

"But will the great medicine man try?"

This time Heyward nodded in agreement, well aware of the stakes involved. Just as he

A Chief Asks the Medicine Man for Help.

and the chief were preparing to leave to visit the sick woman, a long shadow fell across the threshold.

"Le Renard Subtil!" Heyward gasped both in shock and disgust as his enemy stalked into the council chamber.

For a moment, no one spoke as Le Renard sat down on the far end of the log and began to smoke his pipe. Finally, one of the warriors inquired, "Has my friend found the moose?"

"My men stagger under their burden," Le Renard said, glancing around the room for the first time. As he did so, he recognized Uncas, and they eyed each other, like cornered tigers ready to attack.

"It is Uncas, the Mohican!" cried the Iroquois, leaping to his feet. "Mohican, you die!"

The hated but respected name brought all the warriors to their feet. Uncas's quiet smile showed his pleasure at an enemy nation's

Le Renard Stalks In.

high regard for him.

"You Delaware men are squaws!" cried Uncas. "Call out all your Iroquois dogs and let them look upon a brave Mohican warrior, for they all have the blood of cowards."

Le Renard called upon all his powers as an eloquent speech-maker to try to incite the Delawares to join him in revenge. "The sun must shine on his shame," said Le Renard, pointing to Uncas. "Take him to a place where there is silence. Let us see if a Mohican can sleep at night when he is to die in the morning."

Several warriors sprang to their feet and led Uncas away. After the disturbance subsided, the chief who had asked for the aid of the visiting medicine man signaled to Heyward, and the two men left the chamber.

Instead of heading towards the lodges, the Iroquois chief proceeded directly to the foot of a mountain that towered over the village. Small brush fires lighted the path that led up

Uncas Is Sentenced to Death.

the steep incline. At the top, the chief paused and beckoned to the medicine man.

Suddenly, a dark, mysterious-looking being arose in their path. It was a large brown bear, lumbering back and forth, blocking their way and growling fiercely. Heyward knew that bears were frequently tamed by the Indians and lived among them, so he brushed right by the animal. However, the furry beast tagged along behind them, a fact which made the major somewhat uneasy.

After a time, the path came to an abrupt end at the side of the mountain. The Indian shoved open a bark door and led the medicine man through several rooms within a mammoth cave. The bear followed at their heels, growling frequently. In one of the rooms, Heyward found the stricken woman lying on her bed, paralyzed and unconscious, surrounded by a large group of relatives and friends. In the center, trying to create a healing miracle for the dying woman with his

A Growling Bear Blocks the Path.

hymn, was David Gamut.

The Indians had chosen this spot for the stricken woman's care, for they believed that the supernatural powers that victimized her would find it more difficult to attack her through stone walls. In addition, they put great store in the soothing effect of David's hymns and insisted that he sing to her.

As the singing master began his song, Heyward heard strange, human-like sounds directly behind him. Whirling around, he spied the bear crouched down in a corner. Unnerved by the half-human, half-spiritual sounds, Heyward edged closer to David.

But David merely turned and whispered, "She expects you and is at hand." Then suddenly, he was gone.

"David has spoken in English, so his words must have had some hidden meaning," thought Heyward. But he had no time to consider them at length, for the old chief was motioning him to the stricken woman.

David Sings to the Stricken Woman.

"Now," the chief demanded, "the medicine man must show his power."

Trembling inwardly, Heyward approached the patient, but with every step he took, the bear growled savagely.

"He is jealous," said the Iroquois. "I will go now. Take care of her."

As soon as the chief had left, taking the other Indians with him, the most amazing thing happened. The bear waddled up to Heyward and stood up erect like a man. Its body began to shake violently and its huge paws began to pull at its head. Suddenly, the grim head fell off, and in its place appeared the laughing face of Hawkeye!

"Be quiet," cautioned the woodsman. "The savages are everywhere. Any sounds unlike your witchcraft will bring them in here."

"But what are you doing in that outlandish costume?" whispered Heyward.

"I came to rescue Uncas. He was ambushed after you and David left us in the woods.

The Laughing Face of Hawkeye

Then I happened upon one of the medicine men of the tribe dressing for a ritual. A rap over his head gave me his bear finery to carry out my mission. Now, tell me, have you seen Uncas?"

"Yes, he is a captive here and condemned to die at sunrise. Now, what can you tell me of Alice?"

"Don't you recall what David said when he left? He was trying to tell you that Alice is at hand. While this bear was searching for honey, he discovered her in another room. But before you go in and frighten her with all that paint, wash it off in that little spring near the entrance. I will paint you again before we leave."

The reunion between Major Heyward and his beloved was tense and emotional. Alice was so overwhelmed by terror and anxiety that it took all of Heyward's patience to explain to her his plans for their escape. He had no sooner done so when he felt a tap on

Heyward Washes Off the War Paint.

his shoulder. He spun around and, with a sinking heart, glimpsed the evil face of Le Renard Subtil.

"What do you want?" cried Alice.

"Daughter of Munro and white man must die on stake," he bellowed.

Just then, the huge bear stepped forth from the shadows and grabbed Le Renard. Quickly, Hawkeye and Heyward bound and gagged their enemy and left him squirming helplessly on the floor.

As they made their way out of the room, they passed the dying Indian woman. Hawkeye grabbed some blankets and handed them to Heyward. "Wrap Alice in these and listen carefully. Once we're outside, tell the Indian woman's friends that we have locked the evil spirit in the cave and are taking the ill one to the forest in search of medicinal herbs. Remember, I can't say a word, so keep your wits about you, major, and use all your cunning. If you fail, we are as good as dead!"

The Bear Comes Up Behind Le Renard.

Taking the Woman Away from Evil Spirits

CHAPTER 12

A Beaver Joins the Masquerade

As the bear pushed open the bark door, a crowd of babbling Indians descended upon them, eager for news of the poor soul inside the cave. Holding Alice tightly in his arms, Heyward explained to the elder warrior that he was taking the woman into the forest so that his herbs will strengthen her against further attacks by evil spirits.

"But," he warned, "those evil spirits are still locked up in the cave."

"Go!" said the Iroquois chief, who by now had become a firm believer in the medicine man's wisdom. "I will enter the cave and fight the wicked spirits myself."

"Is my brother mad?" cried Heyward "Then the evil spirits will enter you. It would be better to wait until the evil spirits come out and then beat them down with clubs."

The warning had the desired effect. Immediately, the faithful band of relatives and friends settled down under a tree and watched as the three imposters disappeared from view.

As soon as they reached the safety of the forest, Hawkeye gave Heyward directions to a friendly Delaware village. There, they would be safe. Then, bidding his friends farewell, Hawkeye put the bear's head back on and retraced his steps to the Iroquois camp to rescue Uncas.

He located David Gamut's lodge, and once the singing master got over his surprise at a talking bear, Hawkeye enlisted his aid in the escape plan. Together, they slipped quietly through the shadows to the hut that served

Hawkeye Bids His Friends Farewell.

as a temporary prison. As they approached the guards, they were welcomed, for it was well known that their medicine man often wore the skin of the bear.

"Do my brothers wish to see Uncas weep on the stake before his enemies?" David asked knowing full well that the savages would enjoy seeing such weakness in an enemy they hated and feared.

"Ugh," the savages grunted.

"Then step aside and let this cunning bear blow his magic upon the dog inside."

The Indians drew back a little and motioned to the supposed medicine man to enter. But the bear stayed right where it was, growling menacingly at the guards.

"The cunning one is afraid that his breath will blow upon his Iroquois brothers and take away their courage too," continued David. "You must move farther back."

The Iroquois, who feared that such a misfortune was the worst calamity that could

Getting Past the Iroquois Guards

befall them, fell back out of earshot and allowed the pair to enter.

It was silent and gloomy inside the lodge. Only the light from a dying fire flickered over Uncas who lay in a corner. His hands and feet were bound tightly behind him.

"Cut his hands loose," ordered Hawkeye as they rushed in the room. "And you, Uncas take my bearskin." Hawkeye quickly shed his skin and tossed it to the young brave.

"Now, friend," said Hawkeye to the singing master, "let's you and I exchange clothes. And give me your hymn book and your glasses too. If we meet again in better times you shall have them back. But first, you must decide whether you will go with me or stay in Uncas's place."

"I shall stay and play the part until the game is discovered," David announced firmly.

"Spoken like a man," said Hawkeye. "I will bind your arms and legs so the savages will think we attacked you so we could escape.

Exchanging Clothes

Then when you think we are far enough away, call for help."

Then Hawkeye and Uncas, disguised now as David Gamut and the grizzly bear, filed out past the guards. No one stopped them.

No sooner had the adventurers reached the edge of the forest than loud cries arose from the prison hut. Hastily, the Mohican wiggled from his bearskin. Dropping it under a fir tree, he dashed alongside Hawkeye into the somber darkness of the forest.

The discovery of Uncas's escape brought two hundred outraged Iroquois storming out into the night, all awaiting orders from Le Renard. Should they give chase to the culprits or prepare for battle? But their chief was nowhere to be seen.

At that point, the medicine man from whom Hawkeye had stolen the bearskin returned to the village. After he explained what had happened to him, the chief who had taken Heyward to the cave stepped forth

The Iroquois Storm Out into the Night.

and told his story.

Fearing that there had been some trickery, ten of the wisest chiefs proceeded to the cave. There, to their surprise, they found that the stricken woman was lying in her usual place and had not been carried into the forest. Gasps went up all around as the woman's family realized that they had been deceived.

Deeply troubled, the chief inched closer to the bed and saw that the woman was dead. "The wife of my young brave has left us," he said. "The Great Spirit is angry with his children."

The tragic news was received in solemn silence. After a short pause, a dark-looking object came rolling out of the adjoining room into the very center of the room where they stood. It was Le Renard Subtil, still bound and gagged as Hawkeye had left him. The chiefs immediately set him free.

For hours afterward, the entire tribe deliberated in the council lodge. It was all too

The Deception Is Discovered!

apparent now, as Le Renard recounted the successful scheme of Hawkeye and Major Heyward, that they had all been shamefully and disgracefully tricked. "Revenge! Revenge!" the indignant warriors cried over and over.

Runners were sent out in different directions, and they reported back with word that their enemies had fled to the Delaware camp. Then Le Renard announced his plan. He would lead a small party to the Delaware camp to negotiate peaceably for the prisoners' return. The council roared their unanimous approval. Later, Le Renard gathered twenty fierce-looking Iroquois around him and made other plans with them in secret whispers.

The sun was high in the heavens the next morning when Le Renard's party rode out of camp. But instead of taking the path that led directly to the Delaware village, he guided his men around the beaver pond.

With his robe fluttering in the breeze and his beaver totem held high, Le Renard looked

"Revenge! Revenge!"

very grand as he paused to address those furry creatures who were symbols of his tribe.

"You are my cousins," he called out across the water in a loud voice. "I have protected you from the fur traders, and I promise you my continued support. Be grateful to me, for I am the all-powerful Iroquois chief!"

During the delivery of this extraordinary speech, a large beaver peered through the door of an earthen lodge which the Indians believed to be uninhabited. Le Renard spotted the creature and considered his appearance a favorable omen.

Then, with a wave of his hand, the Iroquois gave the signal to proceed, and the party moved out again. Had they taken the time to look over their shoulders as they entered the forest, they would have seen this same strange beaver walk out of the lodge, erect, and remove his fur mask, only to reveal the features of their dreaded foe, Chingachgook!

Le Renard Speaks to the Beavers.

The Delawares Welcome Le Renard.

CHAPTER 13

The Triumph of a Sly Enemy

The Delaware village was bustling with activity when Le Renard rode in later that day. Women hastily abandoned pots of succotash bubbling on the open fires, and men dropped weapons they were cleaning and repairing as they all rushed to greet their visitor.

In a gesture of friendship, the Iroquois threw up his hands toward heaven, and Hard Heart, the chief of the Delawares, made his way through the crowd to extend a warm welcome. Graciously, he ushered his guest into the council chamber where he sat among the warriors, smoking his pipe and talking.

Eventually, as Le Renard hoped it would, the conversation touched on the massacre at Fort William Henry. The Delawares had not gone on the war path because they did not think it wise. But the conversation gave Le Renard the perfect opportunity to pull out his sack of trinkets stolen from the murdered women and present them to the chiefs. Dazzled by the glittering jewels and gold, the Delawares examined their loot gleefully.

Delighted at this enthusiastic response, Le Renard slyly chose this moment to inquire about Cora.

"She is welcome here," Hard Heart said.

"And how is *La Longue Carabine,* the one who has slain my young men?"

The Delawares were startled at the mention of this famous name. "What does my brother mean?" asked the chief.

"Count your prisoners," Le Renard told him, "and you will find your dreaded enemy among them."

Jewels and Gold for the Chiefs

A long pause followed. The chief consulted with his companions, and messengers were sent to collect other men of the tribe.

When they reassembled, there were nearly a thousand people present for the conference. Their revered chief, the wise and just Tamenund, who by now was over one hundred years old, labored slowly, inch by inch, to his seat. His long robe was of the finest fur. Silver and gold medals from many kings hung on his bony, sunken chest. And covering his long white hair was a glittering band set with jewels and feathers.

Soon, several prisoners, who had been lodged in a hut, were led in. Cora and Alice clung to each other. Heyward stood close by, and Hawkeye was at the rear. Uncas was not among them.

Hard Heart rose and asked, "Which of the prisoners is *La Longue Carabine?*"

Hawkeye stepped forward.

"Take your prisoner and go, Iroquois chief,"

Tamenund, the Revered Delaware Chief

Tamenund said to Le Renard.

Several young braves quickly tied Hawkeye's hands together as Le Renard cast a look of triumph at his prisoner.

Cora, alarmed at this strange turn of events, threw herself at Tamenund's feet and begged for mercy. "Hawkeye has never killed a Delaware," she cried. "You must not listen to this Iroquois monster who poisons your ears with lies to feed his thirst for blood."

"Who are you?" inquired Tamenund.

"A woman of a hated race, but one who has never harmed you or your people. I ask that you be just to all your prisoners. But one has not been brought out with us. He is one of your own people. Hear him speak!"

"He is a snake," a young brave muttered. "We are keeping him for the torture."

"Let me see him," demanded the old chief.

At length, when Uncas stood before him, Tamenund asked, "With what tongue does the prisoner speak?"

Cora Begs For Mercy.

"Like my father, I speak with the tongue of a Delaware, for the Mohican and the Delaware are one nation."

"I have not heard of a Delaware so base as to creep like a poisonous serpent into the camp of his own nation," Tamenund said. "A warrior who deserts his tribe is a traitor. Take him to the fire torture!"

At these words, twenty warriors sprang angrily to their feet and, with their knives gleaming in the air, encircled Uncas. But when they grabbed him, his shirt ripped off and revealed the figure of a small blue tortoise tattooed on his chest.

The braves recoiled in fear, their mouths open and their eyeballs bulging.

"Who are you?" asked Tamenund, rising to his feet and staring at the Indian youth in wonder.

"I am Uncas, son of Chingachgook, a son of the Great Turtle."

"Ah," said the old chief, "the hour of my

The Tortoise Tattoo Frightens the Braves.

death draws near, and now the son of my brother, the wisest chief of the Mohicans, has come to take my place. Come sit beside me."

"The blood of the turtle has been in our chiefs for generations," said Uncas as he kneeled down. "But all are dead now except Chingachgook and his son."

"It is true," Tamenund told his people. "Our wise men have often said that two warriors of our race were in the hills of the white man. And now Uncas has come home."

"Yes, my uncle," replied Uncas, "and with the help of a just man and a friend of the Delaware. He is called Hawkeye, for his sight never fails. But the Iroquois call him 'The Long Rifle' because of the death he gives their warriors."

"Then untie him," said the old chief.

When Uncas returned to Tamenund's side after freeing Hawkeye, the old chief asked, "My son, does that Iroquois chief have a conqueror's hold over you?"

The Old Chief Welcomes His Nephew.

"He has none."

"Does he have a hold over *La Longue Carabine*?"

"Hawkeye makes fools of the Iroquois. Ask them about the bear who tricked them."

"And what about the stranger and the white maiden who came with him?" inquired Tamenund, referring to Major Heyward and Alice Munro.

"They should be free to go," replied Uncas.

"And the woman that the Iroquois left here?"

"She is mine!" cried Le Renard in triumph. "Mohican, you know that she is mine!"

"It is true," Uncas admitted sadly. "By Indian law, she is his."

Tamenund approached Cora Munro and said gently, "A great warrior wants you for his wife. Go with him. Your race will not end."

"Better a thousand times it should," exclaimed the horror-struck Cora, "than meet

Le Renard Claims Cora as His Own.

with such degradation!"

At this point Tamenund turned to Le Renard. "An unwilling maiden makes an unhappy wigwam," he said.

"She is mine!" Le Renard screamed in a frenzy. "Let Tamenund give the order."

"Wait, Le Renard!" cried Duncan Heyward. "Have mercy! Cora's ransom will make you rich. We will fill your wigwam with gold, silver, lead, and powder."

"I am strong without them," cried the determined Iroquois, pounding his chest. "Now I have my revenge!"

"Mighty Tamenund," implored Hawkeye, who saw the frantic looks on the faces of his companions. "Let me go in her place. The Iroquois would rejoice to have me as their prisoner."

"I have spoken," said the chief firmly. "The Great Spirit forbids me to go back on my word."

Hearing the Delaware's final words, Le

Heyward Tries To Ransom Cora.

Renard seized Cora by the arm. "Come," he said. "We will go to empty wigwam."

Heyward rushed up to Le Renard and shook his fist in the savage's face. "These Delawares have their laws that forbid them to detain you," he cried, "but I have no such obligation."

"The woods are open," Le Renard replied coldly. "You may journey where you like."

"Hold it!" yelled Hawkeye, yanking Heyward away. "He'll lead you into an ambush."

"He is right," Uncas told the major. Then, turning to Le Renard, he added, "Go, Iroquois! But when the sun is straight above the trees, there will be men on your trail."

"We are off," cried Le Renard, shaking his fist at the crowd. "Dogs, rabbits, and thieves, I spit on you!"

With these biting words, the victorious Iroquois and his pale, shaken captive rode off into the forest under the protection of the rigid laws of the Delaware tribe.

Le Renard Rides Off with Cora.

Stripping the Bark and Branches from a Tree

CHAPTER 14

Uncas Leads His Nation to Victory

As long as Le Renard and Cora were in view, the Delawares remained motionless, as if charmed to the spot by some magic spell. However, the minute the colors of the Englishwoman's dress blended into the foliage of the forest, the crowd separated.

Uncas hurried back into the lodge where he had been held prisoner. Outside, an agitated group of warriors awaited the appearance of their new, young leader.

First, six braves in war paint emerged from the lodge. They quickly stripped the bark and branches from a dwarf pine that grew in the crevices of a rock and painted the naked trunk with dark red stripes. These were signs of war. Finally, Uncas himself emerged and launched into a long, primitive war dance around the post, raising his voice in a wild chant as he danced.

Other warriors, with faces as dark and menacing as thunder clouds, joined the ritual, chanting wildly until they reached an emotional fever pitch. The rites ended abruptly when Uncas hurled his tomahawk into the post. This act declared him chief of the expedition to rescue Cora Munro.

This act was also a signal for the warriors to split the tree apart with axes and knives. It was a declaration of war by the Delaware nation!

"It's time to move out," cried Uncas, noting the sun's position in the sky. "Our truce with the Iroquois has come to an end."

And so it was that late that afternoon, two hundred eager Delawares led by Uncas,

A Declaration of War!

Hawkeye, and Heyward plowed into the wilderness, knowing full well that somewhere in that forest Le Renard's savages lay waiting for them.

They had only gone a short distance when a lone man was seen advancing toward them with such haste that they thought he might be a messenger from Le Renard, coming with surrender terms. A few hundred yards to their right, he stopped and hesitated for a moment.

"Hawkeye," said Uncas, "he must never report back to the Iroquois."

Hawkeye raised his rifle, then lowered it again. His body shook with laughter. "Uncas," he cried over his shoulder, "it's David Gamut!"

"Have you seen the Iroquois?" yelled Hawkeye as the singer drew near.

"They are everywhere," said David, waving his arms in despair. "And they are up to no good. I had to leave the village because of all

David Comes with a Warning.

the howling and revelry, but even the woods between here and their village are full of them in great force. Perhaps it would be wise to turn back."

"And where is Le Renard?" asked Uncas.

"He has hidden Cora Munro in that cave up in the mountain, and is now leading his savages this way."

"There must be something we can do to help her," interrupted Major Heyward.

"I have a plan," Hawkeye told them. "Give me twenty men, and I will proceed along the stream to the beaver pond. There, I will join forces with Chingachgook and Colonel Munro. I shall signal you with one whoop, and we shall deal our enemy a blow that I promise you will make their line bend like a bow. After that, we shall take the village and release Cora."

"I approve of your strategy wholeheartedly," said Heyward. "Let's get started."

Major Heyward had every reason to

Hawkeye Reveals His Plan.

applaud Hawkeye's scheme because it turned out to be amazingly successful. The Iroquois attack, when it finally came, was fierce and desperate. However, their braves were simply no match against Hawkeye's experience and Uncas's skillful leadership. Those Iroquois who weren't killed scattered into the forest.

When Le Renard saw the lifeless bodies of his comrades strewn all over the ground, he cowardly slipped away too, accompanied by two of his loyal braves. Uncas spotted them just as they sneaked into a nearby thicket and raced up the path that led to the base of the mountain.

Le Renard led his determined pursuers on a wild chase as he tore up the steep incline and disappeared into the mouth of the cave. Uncas and his party dashed into the long and narrow entrance after them—just in time to catch a glimpse of the retreating forms of the Iroquois.

Rushing through the dark, gloomy passages

Le Renard Escapes.

and subterranean rooms of the mysterious cave, Uncas kept his eye on Le Renard as if his only purpose in life was this savage's scalp. Heyward and Hawkeye pressed on behind him.

The way had become more rugged and intricate, and it soon seemed as if they had lost the warriors completely. Suddenly, they spotted a fluttering white robe in the passage ahead.

"It's Cora!" cried Heyward, horrified and delighted at the same time.

"Have courage, dear lady," cried Hawkeye. "We are coming!"

Although they now ran faster, the path soon narrowed, becoming nearly impassable. When Uncas and Heyward foolishly abandoned their rifles and leaped ahead, Le Renard turned and fired, wounding Uncas in the shoulder.

"We must get closer," said Hawkeye, leaping past his friends. "Otherwise they will

Wounding Cora's Rescuers

pick us off one by one. See, already they are using Cora as a shield."

As he spoke, Cora disappeared with her captors into an opening in the roof of the cave. "I will go no farther," she cried, stepping unexpectedly onto a dangerous ledge near the top of the mountain. "Kill me if you will, detestable Iroquois, but I will go no farther."

Le Renard drew his knife impatiently. "Woman," he said, "choose! Either my wigwam or my knife."

When Cora didn't reply, Le Renard lifted his knife again. But suddenly, out of the darkness above, a piercing cry was heard. Uncas leaped frantically from a ledge and landed squarely in front of Le Renard. As the Iroquois chief recoiled in shock, one of his warriors finished what Le Renard had threatened. He plunged a gleaming knife into Cora Munro's heart!

A Senseless Murder!

Le Renard Stabs Uncas.

CHAPTER 15

The Last of the Mohicans

The last thing Le Renard wanted was the death of Colonel Munro's eldest daughter. Their marriage would have been the sweetest revenge he could have against her father.

Therefore, Cora's senseless murder drove him into such a state of madness that he immediately leaped for her killer. But Uncas was standing between the two Iroquois, gazing in frozen horror at Cora's murderer. Seeing a more hated enemy with his back to him, Le Renard buried his knife in the Mohican's back.

Like a wounded panther turning on his foe,

Uncas arose and, with the last of his strength, struck Cora's murderer dead at his feet. Then he turned to Le Renard with hate and anguish in his eyes. But the Iroquois seized the limp arm of the Mohican and drove his knife three times into his chest. The proud young chief fell dead at the feet of his ruthless enemy.

By this time, Heyward and Hawkeye had mastered the dangerous crags and arrived at the ledge just above the death scene. Peering down, the major shouted, "Murderer!"

The jubilant Iroquois uttered a cry so fierce and wild that it could be heard in the valley a few thousand feet below. Then, hurling his bloody knife at Heyward, but missing, he turned and hurried along the narrow, winding path that led farther up the mountain.

Hawkeye and Heyward, only minutes behind Le Renard, saw the savage pause and hesitate on the very edge of the dizzy height. As Hawkeye raised his rifle and took aim, Le

Le Renard Hurls His Knife at Heyward.

Renard sent a large rock tumbling down the path, then prepared to leap over the crevice to a point where he could not be reached.

Laughing hoarsely, he made a desperate leap. But his feet fell short of his mark, although his hand grasped a bush on the side of the mountain.

Hawkeye raised his rifle and shot, at the same moment that the bush tore itself out of the soft dirt. Le Renard loosened his hold and his body cut the air, heading downward to death below!

The tragic news of the death of Uncas and Cora sent the whole Delaware village into deep mourning. There were no shouts of success or songs of triumph as a result of their victory over the Iroquois. Pride and celebration were replaced by grief and silence as the tribe prepared for the funeral ceremonies.

Shortly after dawn the next morning, six Delaware girls began scattering sweetscented herbs and forest flowers on the litter that

Hawkeye Shoots As the Bush Tears Loose.

carried the body of the brave and high-spirited Cora Munro. She had been clothed in the finest Indian robe in the village. At her feet sat her desolate father and sister, while David Gamut and Duncan Heyward stood nearby, the one reading a prayer from his hymn book, the other fighting to hold back unmanly tears.

On another litter lay the body of the brave chief Uncas, adorned with the most gorgeous ornaments that the wealth of the tribe could furnish. Rich plumes nodded above his head, and wampum, bracelets, and medals adorned his body. Like Colonel Munro, Chingachgook stood beside the corpse, gazing steadily on the cold, lifeless face of his son.

Then, Tamenund, who occupied a place only a few feet away, arose and addressed his people. "The face of the Great Spirit is behind a cloud," he told them sorrowfully. "His eye is turned away from you. His ears are shut. His tongue gives no answer."

Prayers for Cora

As their leader spoke these terrible words, a low murmur of voices began a chant in honor of the dead. The sounds were those of females, soft wailing sounds.

One Indian girl, selected for the task by her rank and qualifications, delivered a eulogy for Uncas. "He was the panther of our tribe," she cried. "His moccasin left no trail in the dew. His bound was like the leap of a young fawn. His eye was brighter than a star in a dark night. And his voice in battle was as loud as the thunder of the Great Spirit."

She went on to speak tenderly of Cora and asked the Great Spirit to be kind to her. She spoke of Cora's matchless beauty and noble character.

The Delawares listened like charmed men, with deep sympathy showing on every face.

A signal was given by one of the elder chiefs to the women. They lifted Cora's bier and advanced slowly, chanting all the while.

David whispered to Colonel Munro, "They

A Eulogy for Uncas

move with the remains of your child. Shouldn't we follow and see that she has a Christian burial?"

Munro rose and, along with Alice, trudged sadly after the simple procession to a secluded knoll. There, Cora Munro was laid to rest in the soft earth, surrounded by young, healthy pines.

The Indian girls hesitated, hoping that the ceremony suited Cora's family.

Then Hawkeye spoke up in their native language. "My daughters have done well. The white man thanks you." Then, glancing at David who was thumbing through his hymn book, he added, "I see that one who knows the Christian way is about to speak."

As the singing master led the hymn, the Indian women listened spellbound, as if they actually knew the meaning of the strange words. When the ceremony was over, they slipped quietly away.

"My daughter's death is the will of God, and

A Christian Burial for Cora

I submit to it," said Colonel Munro, taking his leave. "Come, gentlemen. Our duty here is ended. Let us depart."

As he mounted his horse, he took one last fleeting look at the little grave, and then he, Heyward, Alice, and David passed before the Delawares and were soon deep in the forest.

Hawkeye returned to Chingachgook's side just in time to catch a parting glance at Uncas whom the chiefs were enclosing in his last robe of animal skins. They paused to permit Hawkeye one last, lingering gaze at his friend. Then came a procession like the other, and the whole nation collected around the grave where the young chief was buried with his implements of war.

After this second ritual was over, Chingachgook was expected to speak to the tribe. Looking into the faces of the dejected warriors, he said, "Why do you weep? Because a young man has gone to the happy hunting grounds? Because he was a chief who filled

Uncas's Funeral Procession

his time with honor? He was good. He was brave. Our Great Spirit needed such a warrior and has called him away. And I, his father, am alone."

"No, no," cried Hawkeye, stretching forth his hand in friendship. "The colors of our skin may be different, but God has placed us so we will journey in the same path. I, too, have no kin, but I felt as close to him as if he were my brother. He fought by my side in war and slept by my side in peace. The boy may have left us, but you, Chingachgook, are not alone."

Chingachgook grasped Hawkeye's hand in friendship, and the scalding tears of the two men watered Uncas's grave like drops of falling rain.

For years afterward, as these two sturdy woodsmen prowled the forests of the New World together, they never forgot the deep ties of brotherhood that had taken root on the grave of Uncas, the last of the Mohicans.

The Deep Ties of Brotherhood Take Root.